SONG OF THE SEA

Lucien Nolan

Copyright

All rights reserved. No part of this publication may be reproduced, distributed, or transmitted in any form or by any means, including photocopying, recording, or other electronic or mechanical methods, without the prior written permission of the publisher, except in the case of brief quotations embodied in critical reviews and certain other noncommercial uses permitted by copyright law.

Copyright © Spaztastic, 2022.

Table of Contents

Chapter One: Hush Now, Mo Stóirín

'Captain Treader, came the familiar knock that resounded through the room and awoke the head that housed short, curled, fire-red locks.

The owner of the tresses had a severe face about her, with sharp eyes and a lean form to match. She would be regarded as a typical sort of pretty if not for the intimidation that she pushed on those who worked under her and the scars that crossed her features angrily, whether it be from battles or fights she had picked in her younger years that went awry. Despite this, she had a confidence that was uncommon of a woman in the lands from which she hailed, but the men who served as her crew had nothing but the utmost respect for her and as she stood, tucking her loose tunic into her trousers, the waistline of which meeting about an inch below her navel, she called back in a gruff voice.

"A moment!"

A patient silence rested on the opposite side of the door and she knew it was King Caspian X who awaited as she slid her boots onto her feet. He was her employer, the king of the Telmarine people in search of his father's council to bring them back to their homes. Caspian was one of the handsome men she had worked under, with shoulder-length dark locks and warm, kind brown eyes, and a tasteful stubble on his cheeks. Dawn Kerrigan Treader, whom her father had named her ship after in her youth, enjoyed working under Caspian and despite having spent the greater part of her life upholding her father's pirating ways, she would gladly serve under him for any time longer.

She preferred the name Kerrigan and very few people called her by that name, one of them being the man that awaited her as she pulled the door open, "I suppose there's a sufficient reason for you waking me when my dear friend Drinian is more than capable"

"I've got some people I'd like you to meet, Caspian nodded eagerly, Kerrigan then noticing that he was soaked head to toe.

"Well, let's see them then," she sighed, knowing best that oftentimes it was easier to do as Caspian pleased.

He grinned a beaming smile and clutched a bundle of clothes in his hands. The pair started out into the shining sun of the upper deck when Kerrigan heard the cries of a boy, a young one, pleading for someone or something to get off of him. For the boy's sake, she prayed this was not who Caspian wanted her to meet, he was not Impressing her, especially when she saw what he was protesting

"Reepicheep! Stand down!" she ordered, watching the large mouse stand at attention and back himself away, staying his blade

"So sorry, Captain." Reepicheep apologized briskly, then spotted those that Caspian led her to, greeting them fondly, "Your majesties.

"Hello, Reep, what a pleasure," another soaked form chuckled endearingly.

Aside from the boy that still lay squirming and whining on the deck, his hair fair and face spattered with freckles, there were two others who were not a part of her crew. They were soaked, like Caspian and two other members of the crew and as Kerrigan looked them over, she felt as if they looked oddly familiar. The boy, who was about the age of our young Captain, had a head of raven hair and matching dark eyes, that were lit up at the greeting of his old friend, while the girl had an air of childlike innocence that filled her soft blue eyes and was portrayed by her long, flowing chocolate locks. They were both in a garb that differed from that of the former pirates and their captain, but it made Kerrigan more curious than anything.

"That giant rat thing just tried to claw my face off!" cried the blonde-haired boy who was sopping wet from head to toe.

"I was merely trying to expel the water from your lungs, sir," Reepicheep answered honestly and simply

"It talked!" exclaimed the male to whom he spoke, "Did anyone just hear that? It just talked!"

"He always talks," answered Kerrigan with slightly narrowed eyes, confusion on her face.

"Actually it's trying to get him to shut up that's the trick," Caspian added and after a brief laugh, Kerrigan turned her attention to the newcomers aboard her vessel. He watched her size them up, then gave his throat a clear before speaking, "Captain Kerrigan Treader, this is King Edmund, the Just, and Queen Lucy, the Valiant."

"Ah," Kerrigan answered shortly, raising her chin momentarily before she heard a thump as the other boy fell to the ground after seeing their Minotaur friend, Jemain. Such only prompted her eyes to roll indignantly as she turned to Caspian, "Your friends are welcome here so long as they keep out of my way. Is that clear?"

The brows of not only Caspian but Lucy and Edmund rose. Edmund and Lucy hadn't expected her to blatantly disregard their titles, nor had they expected her to be so coarse, to which Caspian replied lowly:

"Kerrigan, please, show some respect."

"You know I don't care for titles," Kerrigan spoke sharply to Caspian, her voice somewhat low, "And I do not answer to Kings or Queens that have given me no confidence nor a reason to put any stake in them and I've got my king, I do not need another." Before he could part his lips to reply, Caspian was brushed off and Kerrigan turned to her assistant Captain, "Drinian, this will be your dealings."

As Kerrigan disappeared back into her quarters, Caspian sighed over his shoulder, "She's really quite sweet."

"I can see that," Edmund muttered and shook his head.

Chapter Two: Close Your Eyes and Sleep

"You could have been a bit more welcoming," Caspian sighed, tossing the door shut behind him.

The night had rolled in and out with a fierceness, leaving Kerrigan to sit in her room, longing for her typical quarters. She had given the room over to Caspian upon his fulfilling her debt, but she still missed the lovely room with greatness. The room she had taken up was just below it, with less of a wonderful view and smaller than she cared for Her desk was much less fine and the bed far stiffer, but she bit her tongue on those matters and allowed Caspian to invade her space and sit on the one piece of furniture that she had brought down with her

"I'm sure if I had faked it, I could have been quite convincing, but I owe nothing to either of them," she waved a hand, playing with a jeweled dagger.

"You owe nothing to anyone," Caspian sighed, "Your debt has been paid Kerrigan. You've given more to me than I could have ever asked, but as your friend, I ask that you show them why I love you,"

She glanced at him with a sideways glare and huffed out a breath, "Flattery will get you nowhere."

"Liar," he smirked.

Kerrigan chuckled gently before rising from her cot, sauntering smoothly towards him. Caspian knew the look in her eyes well, hardly missing a beat as she grabbed the cutlass from her desk. He grabbed the first spare blade he could find and poised it just so, a glint of mischief in his eyes.

"If I win, you'll be more friendly," Caspian bargained

"And when I win?" Kerrigan taunted

"I'll leave you be."

"Deal"

He made the first slash. She parried with ease and turned away, throwing her elbow out as she yanked open the door behind them. They carried on fighting, a choreography taking on the motions, but their styles were different. Caspian had been taught to fight like a royal, but Kerrigan had learned to fight like a soldier, then a sell-sword, and finally a pirate. She was brutal where he had finesse; he was careful where she was quick on her feet. They were both well-trained in their own right, but Kerrigan was not afraid to fight dirty.

"Come on "Treader!" some of her crew belted out.

She grinned with such a might that it should have made those around them a bit afraid, but when she struck the butt of her sword against his hand, she caught it quickly and ended the match. Caspian, though his lip was split, smiled at her and wiped the bit of blood from his chin

"Go on then, be a hermit," Caspian conceded

"With pleasure," Kerrigan bowed, inciting a
wave of laughter.

She surveyed the men - the family- that she had
gained over the years, giving them a soft smile.
Her eyes fell upon the three strangers that had
taken up residence in her ship and her smile
fell, straightening back into the stony
expression once more. Kerrigan's eyes fell upon
Edmund, who had been smiling at her prowess,
and she surveyed his features before turning
away and making her way to her quarters.

"Can I have a go?" Edmund called down the
deck.

Caspian bit down the inklings of a smile. He
knew his friend couldn't turn down a challenge
when it looked her in the face, and this would
be no different. She licked her lips and turned,
squinting at the young king.

"I wouldn't want to risk your pretty face, your
majesty," Kerrigan mocked.

"Sounds like you're scared."

Her face grew hard. Caspian stepped back from her, and Kerrigan spun her cutlass. She flourished the blade and waited for Edmund to match her stance.

"I should warn you," Caspian called, "She fights dirty."

Kerrigan gave a smirk that sent a peculiar sort of chill down Edmund's spine. He steadied the blade in hand and waited. They stood, watching, and gauging each other for a moment before she struck down the front and hard. Edmund blocked the blow and before he could even process what was happening next, she had rolled beneath his left arm and struck again. He turned just quick enough to prevent what might have been a killing blow, and the two began trading blows and blocking the best they could.

As Edmund thrust forward, Kerrigan grabbed forward, wrapping her left hand around the blade, and pulling it forward. He jerked into her, and she pointed the tip of her blade up towards his neck, watching as Edmund swallowed hard. He nodded gently and she released the blade, flexing her hand slightly.

"I don't fight dirty," Kerrigan stated, her blade still close to cutting his throat, "I'm just not afraid to take risks."

With that, she removed her blade and patted Edmund's shoulder. The feeling of her hand on him, even through the cloth of his shirt, made him bristle. As she made her way to Drinian, she called aloud a command that made all perk up:

"Land ho!"

Chapter Three: Waltzing the Waves

Kerrigan flexed her hand, inspecting the red lines that Edmund's sword had made upon her grabbing the blade. It had been an action in the heat of battle, but the look on Edmund's face when she bested him was well worth the bit of discomfort. He had been primarily shocked, then utterly impressed, and since that moment, he had begun watching her every move

As they stood at the helm, Caspian on her left and Edmund on her right, she savored the way that the latter

seemed hesitant to talk. It brought her great comfort to finally have some peace and quiet.

"The Lone Islands," Kerrigan exhaled, passing the monocular telescope to Caspian, "the port of

Narrowhaven.

"Strange, not a Narnian flag in sight," Caspian remarked.

Caspian passed the telescope to Kerrigan, and she handed it off to Edmund, glancing at him briefly. In that passing moment, she noted the way his throat tightly bobble and when their hands brushed, he flushed. Kerrigan narrowed her eyes thoughtfully before turning away and pressing her hands against the railing of the ship with care

Edmund cleared his throat carefully and exhaled, "But the Lone Islands have always been Narnia's." Kerrigan turned her nose up at the strangeness of it all; Edmund added, "I say we preparc a landing party"

The flaming redhead turned her eyes to Caspian. She waited for his command with patience, though she

could feel Edmund's impatience rising silently. The long-haired king gave a low nod and Kerrigan cleared her throat.

"We'll use the longboats then," she exhaled then turned over her shoulder, "Drinian, choose men to go ashore You'll be in charge at landing."

"Aye," Drinian replied.

"Tavros," Kerrigan turned upon the minotaur, giving a quick nod.

"Yes, Captain" Tavros confirmed, turning her attention to the deck, "Man the longboats, furl the sail and prepare to drop anchor!"

"You're not coming ashore?" Edmund questioned, his brow raising.

Kerrigan only spared him half a glance before heading down the stairs to the lower deck. Caspian followed her into her quarters, keeping close behind her. She could feel him burning up her trail, but until he shut the door behind them, neither spoke.

"Kerrigan," Caspian sighed.

"Yes?" she hummed, grabbing a map from her desk, and inspecting it.

"You could've been nicer," the young king remarked.

"And why would I do that?" she raised a brow, glancing back:

"Because he likes you."

Kerrigan froze at the statement. She placed the map down slowly and exhaled a deep, careful breath. Caspian stood behind her, arms crossed over his chest and as she turned slowly, he waited. Her shoulders were taut, her fingers curling around the edge of the desk as she faced him. To anyone who knew her less, her eyes were nothing short of murderous, but Caspian could tell she was guarding something.

"I'm not a plaything," Kerrigan spoke slowly

Caspian exhaled slowly and lowered his gaze before he spoke again, "I know that Kerrigan...but we are not in Archenland anymore. You don't have to be so wary of affection."

She swallowed the lump in her throat with increasing difficulty, "You should get ready to board."

He pressed his eyes together and sighed but conceded. As the young man turned himself to exit, he paused only a moment to glance back at her. Kerrigan turned her back to him again and had started muttering irritably to herself. When the door shut, she looked back, her eyes skimming the door before lowering to the floor. She sighed heavily and shook her head.

When the others did depart, she watched the longboats pull away from the ship, her eyes catching Caspian's as she rubbed the red lines on her palm.

Chapter Four: Diving in the Deep

They had been gone far too long. Kerrigan rubbed her knuckles into her hand as the men sailed them closer, their small group now clad in blue robes to disguise themselves. She rarely left the Dawn Treader, land made her nervous and people made her even more unease. Nonetheless, Caspian and Drinian hadn't come back yet and that was all that mattered.

"Captain," Reepicheep nudged carefully, drawing Kerrigan's eyes upward.

She was the last in the boat besides the noble mouse, who was watching her furrowed brow with care. Kerrigan let out a soft sigh, gesturing for Reep to climb up into her cloak, before stepping up onto the sandstone. The redheaded Captain took the lead, gesturing to the right and left to fan out the men they had brought along. The crew followed her direction with no words passed between them and when they came upon the slave market, she straightened and

placed her hand carefully on the hilt of her
cutlass

"I bid 60!"

"1 bid 80!"

"One hundred for the little lady!*

"One hundred and twenty!"

"One hundred fifty!"

Kerrigan glanced between the bidders with a
firm, unfriendly expression. Lucy stood on the
block, a collar around her neck, and her hands
bound before her. The Captain wanted to cut
the men down as they stood, but she was
waiting for the others to get into position. Those
on the right were in their allotted space, but on
the left, she waited.

They placed the "sold" sign around the young
girl's neck and brought up the other boy.
Kerrigan had heard that his name was Eustace,
but she didn't speak to him and found his voice

to be rather irritating. He bore an expression of indignance, rather than fear, which Kerrigan had to admit was impressive on his part. As he stood upon the block and bickered with his bidders, she and the other men moved closer to the marketplace.

"I'll take him off your hands," Reep called confidently cried, "I'll take them all off your hands!"

With his second remark, Kerrigan cast her cloak from her shoulders and the others followed suit. She brandished her cutlass with a quickness and rushed forth, leading the charge. Reepicheep pursued the auctioneer and freed the captives, while Kerrigan took to giving the men a good, unyielding fight. It was clear that she truly did not fear getting hurt in battle if it served her purpose, as she rolled harshly to the ground and kicked out, taking down a man who had attempted at sneaking up on her.

"Look out!" a sharp cry tore through the sky.

Kerrigan turned and ducked at the same time, slashing out and turning her head away from the spurting blood that splashed her face. She spat and rubbed the side of her face with the back of her hand, then squinted against the sun to let her eyes fall upon Edmund, who had been her savior in that moment. He wore a look of relief that she had heard his cry before it was too late, but Kerrigan's face was less so softened. She saw the masses headed for him and took off, kicking dirt into clouds behind her as she half-ran, half-scurried to the staircase, hacking through those who sought to keep her from Edmund

When she broke through the last man and spotted him, she passed along the second sword on her hip and asked a single question, "Where's Caspian?"

"No idea," he shook his head.

She bit down on the inside of her lip fiercely and decided. She would need to get Edmund and the others out safely before she pursued Caspian's safety. Letting out a hoarse groan, she pulled on his vest and jerked him closer, pulling him along before Edmund could fully gather what was happening. He followed her after the bit of prompting and she hurried down the stairs with him at her back. From her periphery, she saw Caspian's head of flopping locks, the swirling of her stomach finally starting to quell as the finished the battle

When all was said and done and she saw him coming from the depths of the battle, Kerrigan couldn't help the quick shuffle of her feet. She hadn't ever worried for Caspian quite like this and as she approached, it was clear that he had shared her concern. He took her tightly in his arms and squeezed, catching the flaming redhead admittedly off-guard, but she returned the gesture eagerly. Behind him, she saw Drinian, smiling as if he had just won a bet of sorts and could not wait to cash in, but upon looking at him a bit more carefully, she noted that he was looking behind her.

Kerrigan followed his gaze with a squint and landed upon Edmund. His lips were turned and pinched into a frown, one that confirmed what

Caspian confirmed and observed about him. She frowned in response and turned away, observing the cheering masses that had since taken to praising them for their rescue and defeat of the traders. She fell silent beside Caspian, Drinian on her other side and Edmund positioned to the right of Caspian. It was a deliberate placement on her part, both to deter Edmund speaking with her and to be sure that she could protect Caspian.

"Your Majesty! Your Majesty!" a man cried out, rushing forth.

All hands reached for their weapons, but none so swift as Kerrigan, her cutlass unsheathed, and eyes narrowed pointedly. Drinian had already taken a hold of the man before he had reached the captain, but it did not deter the sharp blade poised close to his throat.

"My wife was taken just this morning," he explained.

"Daddy!" a little girl cried out.

Drinian allowed him to approach as Kerrigan's blade lowered, listening to what the man had to say, "I beg you, take me with you."

There was a commotion and Kerrigan quickly gathered that the girl, whom another woman had called Gael, was the man's daughter. He ordered her to stay with her aunt and Kerrigan watched the distraught furrow of the girl's brow as he again pleaded to accompany the crew on this endeavor. Kerrigan looked back to Caspian. The dark-haired king searched her face, trying to get a read on an expression otherwise undecipherable, but she merely gave a short blink, then nodded.

"Of course, you must," Caspian obliged, "Meet our Captain. This is Kerrigan Treader.

"It's a pleasure," the man nodded.

She returned the gesture shortly and hastened her pace, hurrying to prepare the boats. There she found Eustace, fiddling with a paddle as he attempted to figure out how to row himself back to the Treader. He glanced up at her and relaxed ever so slightly, handing the oar over as she silently reached out. Kerrigan stepped down into the boat and notched it into place, then did the same with the other and gestured for him to sit. She turned to helping the others into the ships, alongside supplies that had been granted them.

It was not lost on her when the girl, Gael, climbed into one of the supply containers, but Kerrigan turned her eye to the stowaway and continued on the path she had set forth. When the last of their passengers were loaded, Kerrigan lowered herself onto the rowboat where Lucy, Caspian, and Edmund had boarded. She presumed it was Caspian's doing that the only seat left was beside the dark-haired king, who tucked his hands into themselves the moment she sat beside him. He had the old, crusted over Narnian sword tucked between his legs and when she sat, he turned it over for her inspection. She glanced his way a moment and took it in nimble fingers, inspecting the outer coating with great care.

From her boot, she pulled a small blade and ran it through the surface of the water, coating the sharp end with the unusually sweet Namian water. With care, she notched the tip of the blade into a section of buildup and hammered down with the back of her hand. It chipped off and fell away, revealing a pristine blade just below the surface. She pressed her finger against the cool metal and Edmund leaned closer to inspect the smooth surface, taking in the way her digits trailed along the length.

Chapter Five: Stars are Shining Bright

They had set forth again for their next destination quickly. Kerrigan had been glad to return to the ship and welcome herself home, shuffling through the different floors and directing the new supplies. It felt natural for her to give directions and delegate tasks, but when it was said and done and the day crew had gone to bed, she couldn't help but stay up with the skeleton crew that watched over the ship at night. Rather than taking up her usual post, she leaned over the side railing, watching the waves skip past.

"Shouldn't you be asleep?" a low toned voice inquired, approaching steadily

She glanced back at Edmund, clad in the simple tunic and trousers from that day, his books being the only other addition to his sleepwear. His dark hair was pushed to the side to avoid his eyes and he was chewing on his lower lip in concentration. Kerrigan was sure that it was her lack of sleep that made her eyes linger on his features in the dark. He was looking out at the water, trying not to look at her for what reason, she was not sure, but it was a clear effort.

"Shouldn't you?" she countered, returning her gaze to the seawater.

"Couldn't," he replied, though she could feel his gaze on the side of her face.

Kerrigan turned her head to meet his gaze, narrowing her eyes slightly. It was dark enough that he could barely make out her glare and as they held each other's gaze, she felt a flush in her neck. She wasn't sure if it was unease or embarrassment that burned a trail up and down the back of her neck, but she could not ignore the heat regardless of its source. Kerrigan licked her chapped lips and cleared her throat, nodding once to signify that she too was struggling to find the dream world.

"What troubles your mind, if may ask, Little Prince?" Kerrigan asked, standing straighter and pressing her back against the railing as she gave him a skeptical once over.

"I suppose the same thing that troubles yours," Edmund remarked, attempting to ignore the jab.

"I doubt that," Kerrigan scoffed, pushing off of the railing

Edmund followed her quickly, spinning in front of her. "Then what troubles you?"

Kerrigan rolled her eyes and huffed out a sigh. "You and your sister and your cousin are going to get my ship destroyed. You're going to get my men killed and then you are going to go off to wherever it is you lot disappear to when the day is done."

He frowned at her, "You think very lowly of us."

"You've given me no reason to think otherwise," she remarked, moving to shoulder past him.

Edmund seized her wrist with care, his fingers firm but not overly harsh as they wrapped around her wrist and his face soft and apologetic. Kerrigan, for a fleeting moment, thought that he looked a bit handsome when his face was relaxed like that, and even more so when he smiled, but it was a brief thought that passed and was met with disdain. Quickly, she pulled her wrist away and sneered at him, turning away.

"How can I prove it to you?" he called

Kerrigan glanced back at him, but gave no answer, instead heading to her sleeping quarters with a frightfully hot trail burning up and down her spine.

Chapter Six: Wind is on the Rise

Brooding was something that Kerrigan had become quite adept at. It was something that she had started at sunrise that following morning and would not dispel regardless of Drinian and Caspian's attempts at distracting or brightening her spirits. She brooded into the open seas and glowered at maps, her lips pursed tightly as a fight broke out between the cousin and her beloved Reepicheep. She watched with her arms crossed over her chest, rolling her eyes as the oafish boy clamored into different objects. She knew within these objects remained a stowaway girl waiting to be found and raised her chin, preparing to halt the duel before it led to the girl's harm.

As she descended the steps, Eustace slammed into the covered basket in which the girl remained. It clamored over and she screamed aloud, slowly revealing herself to her father and the crew. Despite her father's surprise, Kerrigan approached the pair and the dark brooding expression of her morning faded into a softer one as she leaned her head slightly.

"I've been wondering when you would make yourself seen, Little Stowaway."

Gael looked up at her with an expression of understanding. She realized suddenly that Kerrigan had seen her

in hiding and said nothing, silently consenting to her presence upon her ship. As her father held her close at her side,

Kerrigan approached the girl and bowed lowly, extending her hand to the little girl as if she were welcoming royalty,

The girl giggled slightly as the fly aways around Kerrigan's face fell in front of her mouth and she blew them away.

losing a bit of her royal inclination.

The young girl took her hand slowly and Kerrigan teasingly curtseyed, enticing Gael to do the same. Once the girl lowered herself as well, Kerrigan straightened and turned their hands sideways. They were shaking hands like sailors suddenly and Gael smiled even wider as Kerrigan remarked

"We may make a Pirate Princess of you yet."

Brushing a strand over the curve of her shoulder, Kerrigan looked to Lucy to take over. The young Queen did as she asked, and Kerrigan called out for the men to get back to work. As she climbed the stairs, Caspian gave her a proud smile and she rolled her eyes before standing at the steering. She watched Lucy show the girl to the quarters they would soon share as Edmund climbed the stairs beside herself and Caspian.

She bristled slightly at Edmund's appearance but turned her attention to peering out of the telescope. On either side of the ship, green lands rose and fell, stealing streams of sunlight as it lowered behind the hills. At the end of the narrow pass stood their target, an island that was unassuming at first glance and as she inspected the coastline, she spoke:

"It looks uninhabited."

"But if the lords followed the mist East, they would have stopped here," Caspian added.

She passed the telescope to Caspian and replied, "Could be a trap."

"Or it could hold some answers," Edmund countered.

Edmund and Kerrigan shared a lingering look. He inspected her face in a way that brought a flush to her ears and cheeks, but Kerrigan looked away quickly, clearing her throat in an attempt to get Caspian to intervene. He closed the telescope and glanced her way, noting the way that red splotches had become printed upon her fair flesh. Though humor enticed Caspian, he pushed it away and gave the kingly reply.

"We'll spend the night on shore, scour the island in the morning." "Aye," Kerrigan nodded as she took the telescope, she noted the laughter in his eyes

She frowned at him and made her way back to the office, setting her telescope on the desk. It hadn't occurred to her that Caspian was following her, but when the door shut a second time, she turned and found her friend standing behind her. He had that idiotic grin on his face, one that made her want to punch him square in the mouth, but instead she drummed her foot against the floor until he finally approached and parted his lips.

"Whatever you are about to say, don't," Kerrigan raised a hand. He grinned and made a motion as if zipping his lips, but his expression made Kerrigan groan, "What?"

"I never thought I would see you blush," Caspian remarked.

"It's sunburn," she countered, "I'm pale, remember?"

"I don't see it now," he exhaled, striding closer in mockery.

She looked to the ground in irritation and relented, "Fine, I was blushing."

"At Edmund," Caspian added, jabbing in a way that he knew would annoy her.

"Says who?" Kerrigan shook her head, "Maybe I was blushing because of you."

"Really?" Caspian chuckled, approaching until he was standing right in front of him.

"Yes," she raised her chin.

"Kiss me then," the young King challenged.

It was a simple challenge, but a challenge, nonetheless. Kerrigan was never one to let such an affront go unaddressed and as he stood before her, she knew that she would have to follow through the deter his snooping. With a quirk of the brow, Kerrigan reminded herself

that she had thought of kissing Caspian before,
which made this an easy challenge to accept.
She swept her hand along his neck in a way that
sent a shiver through the young king he hadn't
expected her to genuinely initiate his challenge,
but her fingers trailing along his nape reminded
him just how long they had been at sea. Caspian
hadn't been with any women on land, but such
was his choice - this isolation was a factor of the
quest.

Kerrigan lifted herself to him, pressing their
lips together. Caspian, despite feeling platonic
adoration for Kerrigan, was suddenly reminded
of the first time he saw her. Her lips on his were
replied with his hands on her hips, running
along her spine and up towards her hair. She
thought of when he had saved her life and
covered her with his cloak, his eyes filled with a
promise of a better life. He was her best friend.

The door thundered open, and they pulled
apart, but it wasn't fast enough. Edmund stood
in the doorframe, his jaw set as he peered at the
pair, his dark gaze lingering on Caspian
spitefully. Kerrigan felt the drop her stomach to

her feet and she pressed the back of her hand against her mouth, clearing her throat expectantly. He glanced at her and softened; his eyes filled with hurt rather than anger.

"We're about to head to shore."

Kerrigan nodded slowly, "Let me know what you find."

"You're not coming?" Caspian furrowed his brow and Edmund frowned deeply.

would both leave.

"I don't do land adventures, the last time was the last time," Kerrigan nodded and turned away, wishing they

Caspian parted with a lingering glance and Edmund stepped aside to let him pass, turning his attention to Kerrigan, "I didn't figure you two were.."

"We're not," she cut him off.

"Oh," Edmund uttered, but it was clear that he didn't believe her.

He turned to leave, and Kerrigan called, "Edmund?"

The young king looked back at her and she inhaled deeply through her nose, before requesting, "Be careful."

Chapter Seven: Whispering Words

Kerrigan ate breakfast facing the island. She had sent Drinian along and made him promise to keep watch over the group while she stayed on the ship, though there was little she could see. The beach was a distance away and once the party climbed up into the wood, she could no longer identify where they were or if they were safe. Hacking her wooden spoon through her morning porridge, she absentmindedly scooped the goo into her mouth and ignored the lack of flavor. She tossed the spoon down after a few moments of impatience and debated taking a ship to the land, but she had slept too little the night before to be of much use to them.

Just when she had decided that she was going to do so, however, she saw the ships return and tossed her bowl aside, scurrying down the stairs. She cast the ropes over the side and helped the crew lift the row boats upwards. When the small vessels reached the right height, she took to helping the returning group over the railing. When she helped Caspian, they shared an awkward, but otherwise unchanged glance, and when she helped Edmund she felt the familiar rush of heat burning its trail up her back. Her neck flushed when their hands met and she was glad that Drinian had started to talk to her about what they had discovered, allowing her to divert her attention.

That was the tactic that she took on for the next few days of sailing - stick to Drinian, look busy, and avoid speaking with Edmund. He most definitely took notice of this feature of their trip, but she was equally distant from Caspian as she debated whether their friendship would recover from the exchange

On the fourteenth night, they sailed into a horrible storm. While she would never admit it to the others, she

was glad for the tempest, it gave her reason to keep busy and not spend time with either of the men. However, on that night, they would need to plan. It was looking bleak, they hadn't found land, and everyone was soaked to the bone or

seasick or both, depending on the individual. Her men didn't get sick often, but the ship also hardly ever tossed and

turned like this on a typical journey.

"So, we're stuck here," Drinian remarked as Kerrigan leaned against the wall, trying not to watch Caspian staring out the window or Edmund staring at her, "At half rations, with food and water for two more weeks, maximum.

"I'm well aware of the situation Drinian," Kerrigan sighed, rubbing her brow, "What would you have us do?"

"Turn back," Drinian challenged, for they had a working relationship such as this, "There is no guarantee that we will see the blue star anytime soon. Not in this storm. Needle in a haystack, trying to find this Ramandu place. We could sail right past it and off the edge of the world"

"It's a good thing the world isn't flat," Kerrigan remarked with a huff, "Look, I understand why you are worried. The men are nervous, but we could turn around and, in this storm, sail the wrong direction. Turning around guarantees nothing except for a loss of time."

The hardness of her gaze told Drinian that the conversation had met its natural end. He swallowed his discontent and nodded, parting quickly as she pushed off the wall. He didn't fear her he had no reason to - but ance her mind was made, there was only one who could change it. When Drinian had left, and it was clear that Kerrigan had no intention to stray from their course, Caspian rose to stand beside her.

"We sail on?" he double-checked.

"Yes," Kerrigan answered shortly. "But take heed, Caspian, the sea can play nasty tricks on the mind."

With her word of warning, she retired to her own quarters and settled in for bed. The stiff coat was unforgiving as she laid down, eyes focused on the ceiling. The ship swayed back and forth until she finally found her way to sleep, her fingers curling around the blanket tugged up to her shoulders. Eyes pressed tightly; Kerrigan found herself lulled into a horrible nightmare.

She was fourteen. Her bright fire red locks had been cut short against her will and she was being watched like some sort of circus freak. Her arms were bruised and scratched, her stomach and back strained from never having a chance to get out of the small pool that had become her home. Her lower half glistened brightly, the glittering color of her scales reflecting the dim light of the room

The door thundered open. She knew it was the man that kept her prisoner, his horrible laugh echoing as she attempted to lower herself from visibility, praying that he would leave her be. She wanted to find her father's ship and return to the open seas. She never wanted to be in the water again but being atop it would provide a security that nothing else had delivered.

"She's a real firecracker you'll find," he spoke, and she knew that her captor was not alone today.

He'd brought another "friend" to visit her - another pig who paid to grope and paw at her tail and her body. She shrunk further into the water until she looked like a predator in the water, and she was nothing short of that. Backing herself to the opposing wall, she waited until the secondary form appeared. He was unspeakably tall with a beard to his knees, though it was tucked into the belt below his great big belly. She grimaced at the look of him, and his scent made her gag, but when her captor left them alone and the man peeled off his jacket, her stomach soured. He was getting into the pool.

The fear struck her spine, and she knew that there was nowhere she could go once he stepped inside, so she would have to fight. When the mammoth of a man stepped into the water, completely nude and making attempts at coaxing her closer, Dawn knew what she had to do.

"Come on pretty thing," he laughed in way that made her feel bile rise into her throat, "Won't you come say hi."

She parted her lips, but it was not a hello that left her mouth. It was a song. A captivating, dangerous song that permeated the man's mind and held him in place. She approached him then and made her first kill. She held him under the water so long that the spell broke and he struggled, but by then it was far too late.

The guards thundered in when they heard the cries.

Kerrigan was swinging in her sleep. Her body fought what her mind saw in her dreams and before she knew it, she was on the deck slashing and bucking against the men she called her family. She came to as her fist collided with Caspian's jaw, the king falling to his back with a look of clear surprise. Kerrigan gasped and gripped onto the arms that held her back, using the toned forearm for support rather than attempting to escape. The heaving of her chest told the men that she was awake and herself again, but those arms still held onto her, and she was glad that they had no let go, for her legs were trembling. Her knees shook as she remembered the way that they had slashed into her tail moments before her legs returned and she ran nakedly into the night.

"Are you alright?" Edmund whispered into her ear, holding her upright.

Her tunic suddenly felt too thin. She had figured one of her men had been restraining her, not the Narnian king. He held her steady until she finally nodded, relishing the sensation of his arm passing across her stomach. She licked her lips and helped Caspian upright, rubbing her face and looking around at the crew who held nothing but concern for her.

"I'm fine," she assured, "I must've been sleepwalking."

"Sleep fighting more like," Caspian grumbled as he rubbed his jaw, "I take it you had a nightmare as well?"

She regarded him carefully before looking at Edmund, who had the same perturbed look on his face. It was clear that she was not the only one who had had her sleep disrupted. Something was nearby - and whatever it was, it didn't take kindly to visitors.

Chapter Eight: Of Long-Lost Lullabies

"Are you sure you won't come ashore?"

Kerrigan glanced over at Edmund as he paused before the rowboat, his fingers drumming the surface as the others climbed in. He held steady in awaiting the answer, but Kerrigan was silently hoping that he might be deterred from awaiting the answer if she stared at him long enough. His dark eyes remained patient and unrelenting

"I don't much like land, she admitted, sniffing shortly, "Nothing good ever happens there."

He smiled softly at her gruff pessimism and Kerrigan frowned at his lack of deterrence. Instead, he moved closer and peered down as the boats continued to be prepped. She refused to move away and admit to her nerves, instead peering out of the corner of her eye at him

"You saved us the last time you came," he
reminded.

"Only because I had to," she shook her head
and glanced over her shoulder, "I'd prefer if you
don't make me have a repeat performance."

"No promises," Edmund remarked. Her gaze
swung to him with a furrowed brow and despite
the nervous shuffling of his feet, he stated,
"Perhaps I like being saved by you!

She inhaled sharply and spun away from him in
a red-faced huff, making her way to her
quarters. Caspian laughed aloud at her from
down the deck, eaming a sharp, violent look.
Edmund glanced to Caspian with an uneasy
look but climbed down onto the boat and
started out. Though neither Edmund nor the
rest of the party could see it Kerrigan watched
them depart. She stared after the boats and
counted the strokes of the paddles, biting down
on the inside of her cheek. When they halted at
the beach, she watched them depart and return,
moving about but never leaving her perch and

more often than not focusing on Edmund
through the telescope when he came into view.

She felt impeccably foolish, staring after a boy a
year her senior, but it didn't keep her from
doing it. When he passed along the beach again,
she released a sigh and forced herself to return
to the deck and busy with helping the other
men clean the wood. Kerrigan refused to be
caught pining after the boy king. She refused to
give him a second thought, even if he had been
exceptionally and irritatingly kind when
tending to her bruised knuckles the other night
He had talked to her until she was calm and
asked no questions about her bad dream.

It didn't matter that she had seen him chatting
with Reep or telling fantastical stories to Gael
or comforting Lucy when she got that worried
furrow in her brow. He was another stuck up
king-he wasn't like Caspian. He would have her
and throw her aside if she let him.

She jabbed her mop at the deck as she chided
herself in silence, but all of that halted when
she head a great shrieking cry. The rowboat

with Drinian and Lucy came back to the ship, and they were brought aboard, but Caspian and Edmund had gone to look for Eustace, who had quite predictably wondered off. Another screech tore through the sky, followed by a bellow of fire behind the mountains.

"All hands on deck!" She cried out as her eyes met Drinian's. Her second-in-command came down to stand beside her as she gave the second command, "Archers, arm yourselves!"

They scrambled to follow her command and Kerrigan ordered them to their positions, their bows and crossbows pointed upwards as the great golden dragon landed atop the ship's mast

"Hold!" Kerrigan ordered, "On my command."

The dragon had flown close but had not burned them, nor attempted to attack. It was strange, unnerving really, but Kerrigan knew better than to rush an attack.

"He'll break the mast!" Drinian reminded.

"He's not attacking!" Kerrigan observed, "Doesn't that strike you as odd?" "It doesn't matter how it strikes me!" Drinian replied sharply.

Before the two could finish their bickering, the dragon loosened his grip on the mast. Reepicheep had driven his slender blade into one of the creature's digits and cast it off, but when it flew towards the island once more. Kerrigan's stomach dropped. Caspian and Edmund were still ashore. She looked down into the water, debating the risk. Many of the men knew what she was, but Caspian did not, nor did the newcomers. Revealing herself was a great risk

to not just herself, but her crew- no other sirens could do as she did.

As the moral dilemma rang through her mind, she was given no choice. The dragon returned, Edmund gripped in its claws, and she decided that it did not matter whether he had attacked before, Edmund was now in trouble. When he

cried out to his sister for help, Kerrigan
dropped her belt and shed her boots

"Captain Treader," Drinian warned, but
Kerrigan had already stripped the smooth,
enchanted, and bejeweled

anklet, settled it into the foot of her boot, and
dove overboard

Her body broke the water with a start, her legs
forming into one entity as she tore through the
waves, her body feeling at home with them.
From above the waves, she looked like a bullet
tearing through the water, and when she arose,
the water came to match her. The nalads
greeted her like an old friend, and she was sure
that if any mermaids came by, they would help
her without a second glance. Focusing her
energy, she raised her hands and sent a great
wave rolling after the dragon, taking care that
the moving water would not affect her ship.

The water sliced at the side of the dragon and
knocked him off-kilter, but he recovered and
ducked low,

disappearing from sight. Kerrigan clenched her jaw and dove low, starting to the night in an attempt to cut off the

dragon. As she rounded the northern side of the island, she sent another shot of pure water and watched the dragon

barrel out of view again. She debated using her voice, but if the dragon would hear it, then so might the crew.

Clearing her throat, she looked back and found that a boat had already started towards the shore. Drinian was aboard, gesturing with a pair of pants in one hand and the anklet the other. Letting out a frustrated growl, she swam towards them and began pushing the boat from behind, if only to make it approach the shore faster. When they ran aground, Drinian tossed the anklet to her and she slipped it over the edge of her fin, moving it further up when her human legs had returned. She dressed quickly and with the privacy that she could muster in the open and by the time that she had gathered herself and was ready to pursue Edmund and the dragon once more, both had returned.

"It's Eustace!" Edmund cried out as they came to a halt.

The moment that his boots collided with the ground, Lucy rushed to her brother. They embraced tightly and when they separated, Kerrigan moved forward. She pulled him in despite herself, surprising Edmund as her arms wrapped around his neck. Though he was confused and a bit red in the face, Edmund held her tightly, allowing his chin to settle against the side of her head. Caspian was confused on this front and a few others, but he couldn't help the stupid little grin that came to his face when they stood, unmoving.

"Are you alright?" she asked, her voice barely above a whisper.

"I'm okay," Edmund nodded, his lips grazing her ear.

When the concern had been quelled and only
embarrassment remained, she pulled away
from Edmund and turned her attention to
Eustace. She hadn't meant to hurt the boy; she
had only meant to protect Edmund. Eustace,
though petulant and persistently annoying, was
still a mere child, only a few years older that
Gael. If she could take pity on the stowaway
girl, she could show some compassion to the
boy turned dragon.

"Here," she remarked as he bit and gnawed at
the cuff on his arm

He regarded her carefully but stretched his
front limb to her as Edmund remarked, "He
must have been tempted by the treasure."

"Well, anyone knows a dragon's treasure is
enchanted," Caspian remarked, then adjusted
when Kerrigan glared at him, "Well, anyone
from here,"

She pulled the golden cuff with a great deep
huff from Eustace and rubbed the tender spot
tenderly. He roared, then lowered his head to

her in thanks and Kerrigan swallowed the dryness in her throat. He was trapped in a

body that was not his own. She could relate to that fear and uncertainty to a degree.

"Is there anyway to change him back?" Edmund asked.

"Not that I know of," Caspian shook his head.

"What about your anklet?" Lucy asked, her attention fixed on Kerrigan.

The set of eyes turned to her. She had gathered that they all now knew the truth of her, but it felt like a

Culolation to have it en openly inquired after Absentmindedly che linaled the anklet in her boot and glanced to Edmund, who hadn't the faintest what they were speaking of. He had returned after her tail was gone and only saw that she had jumped overboard to pursue him and his captor.

"It's specially made for me," Kerrigan answered,
"If we tried it on Eustace, it might only make
the enchantment worse."

As they mulled over this revelation and came to
terms with what this meant, Tavros gave the
cry, "The boats are ready, sire!"

"We can't leave him here alone," Lucy
remarked.

"Well, we can't bring him on board, Your
Majesty," Drinian replied.

"Drinian, take the others and one of the boats
back to the ship, we'll camp here and figure this
out," Kerrigan ordered, finding his tone to grate
on her nerves - his pessimism was typically
matched by her own, but they needed answers,
not more roadblocks.

"But you've no provisions and no means of
staying warm, your majesty," Rhince remarked,
keeping Gael close to her side.

In answer to Rhince's concern, Eustace bellowed a stream of fire unto a log in their center, to which

Reepicheep inquired, "You were saying?"

"We'll have fish for dinner," Kerrigan remarked, removing her boots, "I'll only be a few moments."

Chapter Nine: Oh, Won't You Come with Me

They had taken the news of Kerrigan's true nature with the confusion and disbelief that she had expected. Lucy and Gael had thought it was a most beautiful truth, Eustace had made a huff of understanding for her sudden sympathy. but Caspian and Edmund had not responded in a way desired. Caspian had rose in a rage. As far as he was concerned, she had lied to him for years, keeping secret after secret. He had noticed the strangeness and the signs. but she had always been able to explain it away. Edmund said nothing. He only stared at her in a way that made her feel uneasy and once it was time to eat the dinner she had caught and fixed, Kerrigan made her way from the fire.

She felt strange and lost, like she had been cast out by the silence of her companions. It was precisely what she had feared, their rejection - namely Caspian and Edmund's was like a knife through the gut. Though she didn't want to admit that Edmund's reaction mattered to her, it did. Pressing her lips together, she crossed her arms over her chest and watched the waves. She watched her ship longingly, as if it might reach out and save her from the feelings of distance that had penetrated the bonds that she had come to build.

The sound swished under the boots of another as he drew near. Edmund pressed his arms behind his back

and kept his gaze low, as if he wasn't sure how to bridge the gap that had mounted between them. Kerrigan glanced

over at him, quickly surveying the way that his face caught the moon's light. The dim illumination was cool against his

face, but when she looked at him, all she felt was warmth.

"You jumped into the water to save me," Edmund spoke carefully.

She wasn't sure if it was a question or not, but Kerrigan nodded gently, "Yes."

"You don't like me," he reminded, though his voice had very little conviction in it

"Yes," Kerrigan cleared her throat, looking at him hesitantly, her eyes moving slowly up his face.

Edmund wore a grin. It was a simple little smile, one that taunted and challenged the reply she had given. They both knew that she had told a lie, but Edmund wanted to hear it from her lips. He could just as easily rile her up and get her confess in a moment of fiery anger, but that wouldn't be as a willing admittance.

"You sure about that?" he asked softly, stepping closer until they were shoulder to shoulder

Kerrigan turned away quickly, willing the darkness of the night to conceal the blush that threatened to ensnare her throat and expose the young Captain. A moment of steely silence passed between them, and Edmund knew that the only confession he would get would have to be through a moment of passing irritation. He laughed

inwardly, then looked over at the girl of seventeen.

"Caspian says you're a good kisser," he teased, keeping his gaze straight ahead.

Kerrigan caught the indignance in the bottom of her throat and huffed, "Wouldn't you like to know?"

She refused to be tricked by such a juvenile comment. He licked his bottom lip at the clear challenge that had arisen between them and glanced over to where Caspian had taken to brooding down the shore

"He thinks you have feelings for me," Edmund jeered, "Though think you're afraid to admit that you like him."

Kerrigan clenched her jaw, then snorted, "Not like that."

"You kiss all your friends like that then?" Edmund raised a brow.

Kerrigan frowned deeply and started to walk further down the beach, hoping that if she walked fast enough, he would drop the subject. Edmund however, now thought he had upset her deeply. Picking up his feet, Edmund hurried after her and Kerrigan groaned to herself when he jogged and took hold of her arm.

"What?" she snapped, spinning on him, "What is your problem?"

Edmund swallowed the lump in his throat, "I'm sorry..."

He was rambling his way through an apology, fingers twisting anxiously as the bravado of a cocky playboy melted into an anxious boy. She liked him more when he wasn't trying to get under her skin - though she figured that was par for the course. His eyes skittered from her face to the space above her right shoulder and back again and though she wasn't listening to his stammering, she wanted him to stop. Kerrigan wrapped a hand around the back of his neck. Edmund froze, his eyes broadening to the size of saucers. They remained there for a moment, exchanging breaths and silent stares. Kerrigan inhaled to speak, but before the words could leave her lips, Edmund leaned forward and pressed their lips together.

She inhaled sharply but didn't pull away. Her hand slid to circle around the back of his neck, keeping him steady pressed against her. Edmund's arms wrapped around her, his arms making the shape of her waist feel a bit fuller and more complete.

When Edmund pulled back, his face had run completely hot, flushing the fair skin, and washing away the freckling of his features. His dark eyes were foggy, but she could tell that he had surprised himself by the way he took to licking his lower lip. Kerrigan watched his lips for a moment, but cleared her throat and spoke:

"We should get some rest."

Chapter Ten: Where the Moon is Made of Gold

The blue star stood high and proud in the sky as Kerrigan leaned over the railing of the upper deck, fiddling with the sleeves of her tunic self-consciously. She took great efforts not to let her hazel green eyes wander to Edmund on the deck, where he was standing between Lucy and Gael. He was chatting to them idly, which made it all the harder for Kerrigan not to look at him and inspect the way that the tunic fell loose around his form, giving an extra taper to his waist.

"You're staring at him," Caspian mocked, catching Kerrigan off-guard.

She turned to him sharply, "Are you talking to me now?"

*Depends, do you have any more secrets?" Caspian exhaled, bracing his hands against the railing beside her.

They watched Eustace pull the ship, his wings
flapping strongly. They were making good
headway with his

help, especially now that the wind had
abandoned them.

"I never wanted to lie to you," Kerrigan shook
her head, "I wanted to keep you safe. you knew
that I killed someone. That was never a secret
but it was because he.."

She looked away and brought her arms to cross
over her chest, biting down on the inside of her
cheek. Kerrigan hadn't spoken about the
incident that still burned nightmares through
her chest, and she didn't truthfully want to,
even for Caspian. He had promised that he
would not ask those questions, but within their
answers were the

reasons for her lies.

Caspian placed a hand on her shoulder. She
knew in his silence that he had excused her
from answering Kerrigan inhaled deeply and

looked over at Caspian. In silence, they climbed down from the deck and made their way into the Captain's quarters, where they discussed and worried on the fruitfulness of the mission. Edmund joined them after an hour or two and a fresh awkwardness swept through the room and Kerrigan threw the doors open to the balcony, inhaling the smell of the salt water.

"We can't be sure the other lords made it to Ramandu's Island," Caspian muttered, running his fingers along the handle of one of the blades.

by the ship

"Where else do we have to look?" Kerrigan raised a brow before turning to watch the foamy trails left behind

By nightfall, they found the island which they sought. The island was a landscape painting of cliffsides and ancient, tall trees, the greenery only disrupted by streaming waterfalls that dropped into the ocean. Kerrigan had taken up her perch on the deck again by the time they arrived, her light brown-green gaze taking in the way the light blue of the sky was tinted with pink and orange, the white fluffy clouds floating overhead of Ramandu's island.

"We'll head ashore," Caspian remarked, "Are you coming?"

Kerrigan felt Edmund's gaze lingering over her when the question entered the air, but she nodded, "Let's go."

It caught much of the crew off-guard that she was going to land willingly, but when she climbed into the ship, they knew that she had meant it. She sat beside Edmund and held her hands tightly, her cutlass perched against her hip. When they ran aground, their group began their trek to the heart of the island. She kept her fingers coiled around the handle and let her eyes flicker back and forth, watching Edmund's back with care.

They passed under a grand tree with high setting roots, opening into a clearing. There stood a great stone table with the sides carved beautifully. They were natural and intricate, with the top covered in bounties of food. There stood candles and place settings, all of which was dimmed by the strange twisting roots at the far end. Kerrigan made her way down the table with haste, peeking into the roots and cobwebs, her eyes widening as she realized that these were not, in fact, trees.

"The lords most definitely made it to the island," she remarked, looking back at Caspian.

"How do you know?" he asked.

"Because they never left."

He made his way to her side and looked upon what she did, finding men frozen in time with long hair and even longer beards. They were encased in thorns and their hands were terribly thin, their fingers spindly Caspian thrust Kerrigan behind her, his blade raised, and she followed suit, her cutlass raised with a steady grip. Edmund shined his torch into the face of the man closest to him, carefully inspecting.

"Lord Revillan," Caspian observed, then looked at the next. "Lord Mavromorn." Lucy smoothed the hair of

another away as the young king nodded, "Lord Argoz"

When Lord Argoz released a soft breath, Lucy gasped and drew back. They were breathing. Though the men were not moving, it was clear that they had been under some sort of spell. The thorns were not just an adorment, it was part of this restraining spell

"It's the food!" Caspian cried, enticing Tavros to drop the apple in his grasp.

Kerrigan didn't like the feeling she was getting in this place, but Edmund disrupted her anxiety as he

exclaimed, "It's the stone knife. It's Aslan's table!" With new hope, they retrieved the swords from the lords' sheaths, quickly placing the blades on the table.

They were short one. Though the seventh was missing, the blades began to glow and turn a subtle shade of blue.

"Look!" Lucy cried.

They followed her command and saw that the blue star was no longer so distant. It moved smoothly overhead, casting beams of light over the group. Kerrigan kept her grip on her blade tight and trained it upwards. They followed the ball of light with their eyes until it descended before them, slowly melting into the figure of a fair-haired woman in a white dress. nav

"Travelers of Narnia, welcome," the blue star spoke. The other men bowed, leaving Kerrigan, Edmund, Lucy, and Caspian upright, the blue star raised her hands gently, "Arise. Are you not hungry?"

"Who are you?" Edmund asked in a gob-smacked manner.

Kerrigan looked his way and scowled at the enchanted expression on his face "I'm Liliandil, daughter of Ramandu," the blue star, Liliandil, spoke, "I am your guide."

"You're a star," Caspian observed

Both kings wore looks of utter enrapturement, their eyes trained on the star in a way that burned a jealous fire in Kerrigan's belly. She was more angered by the way Edmund watched the hyper-feminine star-turned-woman than she cared about Caspian's reaction, but it didn't quell the irritation that was rising from her toes.

"You are most beautiful," Caspian remarked.

"I-if it is a distraction for you, I-I can change form," Liliandil offered.

"No," Edmund and Caspian jumped to answer

They shared a look and as Edmund looked at Caspian, he caught the rigid stature of Kerrigan. She turned to look at him slowly, her eyes narrowed venomously. He knew immediately that he was in trouble. Though she hadn't spoken to him since they had kissed on the beach, but he had dreamt of her every night and though she avoided his gaze, her face heated every time they brushed by each other.

"Please, this food is for you," Liliandril waved her arms, "There is enough for all who are welcome at Aslan's table. Always. H-help yourselves."

The men watched Kerrigan for her command. Her jaw was set, and she surveyed the spirit woman with a

sharp gaze. They would not move without her command, a fact that Kerrigan knew.

"What happened to them?" she gestured down the table, not trusting this glowing form.

"These poor men were half mad by the time they reached our shores. They were threatening violence upon each other. Violence is forbidden at the table of Aslan, so they were sent to sleep, Liliandril explained

"Will they ever wake?" Lucy inquired worriedly.

"When all is put right," the spirit guide nodded, "Come, there is little time."

Her crew looked to her again. Kerrigan bit down on her cheek and waved for them to eat. She still had half a crew back on the ship if they were to become frozen like the other men - it was enough to find the other sword and set things right. The young captain refused to move, however, and instead stood with her arms crossed tightly across her breast. The men began to tuck in; Caspian and Lucy followed the beautiful star away from the table, leaving Edmund staring at Kerrigan and Kerrigan glaring at the spirit's back.

"Kerrigan," he spoke calmly, making his way around the table as she fixed her glare unto him.

"What?" she snapped; jaw clenched so tight that he thought he heard a tooth crack.

"You alright?" he asked, grazing his fingers along her elbow gingerly.

She resisted the shudder that coursed through her body at his touch, but it was clear that the contact had had its affect. Edmund smoothed his fingers up and around her forearm, wrapping his hand around it. Kerrigan bit down on her lip, still training a heated gaze on him that displayed her utter displeasure, but Edmund only stepped closer, sliding his hand around to the middle of her back. She self-consciously looked over at the feasting men, none of whom were paying them any mind, but it didn't quell the feeling that she might appear weak.

Edmund followed her gaze and train of thought and spoke softly, "Walk with me."

She glanced back at her crew and did as he bade, keeping his hand in her own as they went. Edmund liked the feeling of her irritably tugging on his fingers, though she was clearly doing so to avoid properly holding his hand. He chuckled when she started rubbing the side of

his knuckle, caught off-guard when he seized
her hand in the privacy of the wood.

"Jealousy suits you," he smiled softly.

Kerrigan snarled at him and stepped closer,
possession in her gaze, "I didn't think you were
so easily taken."

Edmund licked his lips and fiddled with her
fingers, "I'm not. A girl has to insult me
constantly and glare at me all the time to catch
my eye."

She could tell he was making fun of her, but
Kerrigan pulled on his hand yanking him closer.
Edmund stumbled until they were chest to
chest, noses just barely touching. Edmund let
his dark eyes lower to her lips, then back up
again, but Kerrigan hadn't stopped burning
holes into him with her eyes.

"Like that," he whispered, half-smirking.

She let out a gentle laugh, despite herself, and
leaned forward, connecting his lips with hers.

THE END